WELCOME TO
PASSPORT TO READING
A beginning reader's ticket to a brand-new world!

Every book in this program is designed to build read-along and read-alone skills, level by level, through engaging and enriching stories. As the reader turns each page, he or she will become more confident with new vocabulary, sight words, and comprehension.

These PASSPORT TO READING levels will help you choose the perfect book for every reader.

READING TOGETHER
Read short words in simple sentence structures together to begin a reader's journey.

READING OUT LOUD
Encourage developing readers to sound out words in more complex stories with simple vocabulary.

READING INDEPENDENTLY
Newly independent readers gain confidence reading more complex sentences with higher word counts.

READY TO READ MORE
Readers prepare for chapter books with fewer illustrations and longer paragraphs.

This book features sight words from the educator-supported Dolch Sight Words List. This encourages the reader to recognize commonly used vocabulary words, increasing reading speed and fluency.

For more information, please visit lbyr.com/passporttoreading.

Enjoy the journey!

Little, Brown and Company
Hachette Book Group
1290 Avenue of the Americas, New York, NY 10104
Visit us at LBYR.com

First Edition: February 2022

Little, Brown and Company is a division of Hachette Book Group, Inc.
The Little, Brown name and logo are trademarks of Hachette Book Group, Inc.

The publisher is not responsible for websites
(or their content) that are not owned by the publisher.

Library of Congress Control Number: 2020944632

ISBNs: 978-0-316-42929-0 (pbk.), 978-0-316-42928-3 (ebook),
978-0-316-42930-6 (ebook), 978-0-316-42931-3 (ebook)

Printed in the United States of America

CW

10 9 8 7 6 5 4 3 2 1

Passport to Reading titles are leveled by independent reviewers applying the standards developed by Irene Fountas and Gay Su Pinnell in *Matching Books to Readers: Using Leveled Books in Guided Reading*, Heinemann, 1999.

Friends, Foes, and Heroes

by Elle Stephens

LITTLE, BROWN AND COMPANY
New York   Boston

Attention, Miraculous fans!
Look for these words
when you read this book.
Can you spot them all?

fashion

jewels

yo-yo

butterflies

Meet Marinette!
She lives in Paris.
She loves fashion, music,
and Adrien.

Marinette's Miraculous
is a pair of earrings.
It turns her into
a superhero named Ladybug!

Miraculouses are
magic jewels.
They give superpowers
to people who wear them.

Ladybug is fast and strong.
She has a powerful yo-yo.
She uses it to leap, swing around,
and fight evil!

Tikki is a Kwami!

She powers the Ladybug Miraculous.

She is kind and helpful.

Adrien goes to school
with Marinette.
He likes to read, model,
and play video games.

Adrien's ring is a Miraculous.
It turns him into
a superhero named Cat Noir.

Cat Noir can run, jump,
and climb.
He destroys evil
with his Cataclysm superpower!

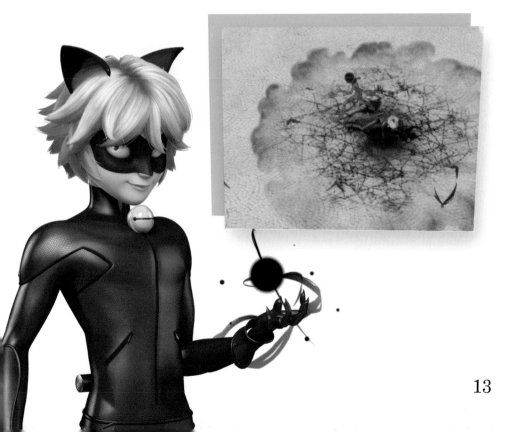

Plagg is Adrien's Kwami.

He powers the Cat Miraculous.

He loves cheese
and playing pranks.

Hawk Moth is
an evil villain.
He wants Ladybug's
and Cat Noir's powers.

Hawk Moth's Miraculous is a pin.
He uses it to create akumas.

Akumas are magical butterflies.
They turn people into evil villains.
Hawk Moth must be stopped!

Hawk Moth's real name
is Gabriel Agreste.
He is a fashion designer
and Adrien's father.

Nooroo is Gabriel's Kwami.

He powers the Butterfly Miraculous.

He is trapped by Hawk Moth.

Alya is Marinette's
best friend.
She is smart, funny,
and a brave reporter.

One time, an akuma turned Alya into
a villain called Lady Wifi.
Lady Wifi wanted to tell everyone
Ladybug's true identity!

Alya's Kwami is named Trixx!
Sometimes, Alya uses a Miraculous
to turn into Rena Rouge.
She is a superhero who
helps Ladybug and Cat Noir.

Nino is Adrien's
best friend.
He loves music.
He wants to be a DJ!

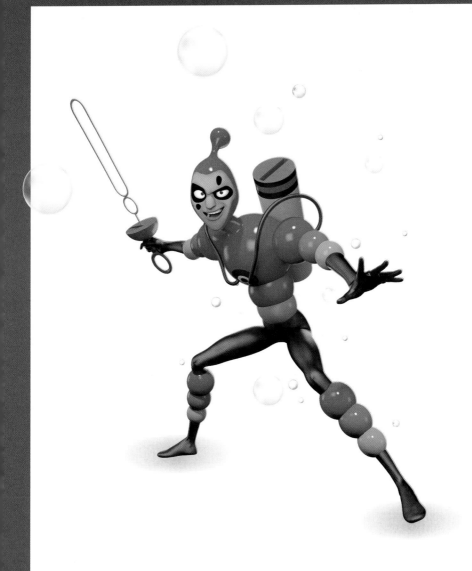

One time, Hawk Moth
turned Nino into the Bubbler.
He was a villain who
trapped people in bubbles.

Nino's Kwami is named Wayzz!
Sometimes, Nino uses a Miraculous
to turn into Carapace.
He is a turtle superhero!
He helps Ladybug and Cat Noir, too.

Chloé goes to school
with Marinette and Adrien.
She is rich, bossy,
and mean to her classmates.

Once, an akuma turned Chloé into
a villain called Antibug.
Hawk Moth wanted her
to stop Ladybug.

Pollen is Chloé's Kwami!
With a Miraculous,
Chloé turns into Queen Bee.
She is a superhero
who fights with venom.

Nathalie works
for Adrien's father.
She takes care
of Adrien.

Nathalie's Kwami is Duusu.
Sometimes, Nathalie
turns into Mayura.
She is a villain
who helps Hawk Moth.

Wang Fu keeps the Miraculouses safe.

He saw how kind Marinette and Adrien are.

He chose them to become
Ladybug and Cat Noir.

These superheroes
are Miraculous!

BE YOUR SELF

Super HEROEZ TEAM

I AM my own HERO

LADYBUG